Little Ms Willow…A short story

I0548587

By Eddie J Martin

About The Author:

Eddie Martin is a retired Air Force Sgt., who lives in Conroe Texas and has been writing for 3 years. Eddie has written a total of 12 books. 3 of his memoirs, 8 fiction and one children's book.

Part 1

That's a beautiful baby, is she yours? A young servicemen asked an older gentleman standing next to him in the nursery room, a newborn baby held in the arms of hospital staff.

Yes it is, our 1st, we've been trying to conceive for over ten years now. Robert said. We had three miscarriages and this is the 1st one carried to term. How old is your wife the servicemen asked? Robert should have taken offense to the question but he said, she's 38 and felt life was passing her by but this baby I think will make up for everything we've lost. She'll want for nothing and we're at the place in our life now when we can give her just about everything.

What type of job do you have, the servicemen asked?

I'm a city bus driver and my wife is a custodian. By the way my name is Robert and my wife name is Joyce, we've named our daughter Janice. Janice Baca willow (Little Miss Willow.) Two days later Robert, Joyce and little Janice departed the hospital for home. Janice had her own room waiting for her, bed, toys and special wallpaper in pink. Rocking chair and floor pads. Janice grew like overnight as all kids seem to do, the ones and twos came and went without any problems. Having a child was about as joyful as Robert and Joyce knew it would be and they just love Janice to death. By all appearances it was one happy family, but then it happened, gradually. It started with a small kitten. Joyce found on their doorstep and told Janice she could keep it, Janice told her mother that she didn't want it. Her mother insisted she knew better and forced the kitten on Janice. The mother bought food, water dish, and bed to teach Janice to take care of it. When Janice was forced to hold the kitten she would squeeze it so tight the kitten would jump out of her hands and run away, this happen Numerous times. And once the kitten went underneath the house and wooden come out, Frightened! And then One morning Joyce found the kitten dead in the backyard. She couldn't find any marks on it but she did ask Janice did she hurt the kitten, she said no.She didn.t know what happen to Kitty and start crying. Joyce didn't too much believe her but she just did not want to believe Janice would hurt the kitten but that was the end of her taking in kittens. The next incident was when Janice was five years old, there was this puppy. Her mother thought she love that puppy so she told Janice she could keep him, two months later he came up missing and was never seen again. During that same time a bird had fell out of there tree, its wing injured. Janice found it and told her mother she would take care of it, two days later the bird was found in a paper bag and the bag had been set on fire.

At seven Janice was given a rabbit for Easter by her aunt. Everyone believed she loved the rabbit so much because for a while they were insatiable, the rabbit was found a week later all bloodied in its cage, one of its legs pulled off, dead.

No one could ever find out what happened, no one said what they thought but everyone knew. Janice was asked what happen to the rabbit and she swear that she didnt know. She said she think the mean man did it.

One afternoon one of Janice school mates fell in the creek and drown, he was seven years old. They were both together playing when it happened. Janice said he slipped and fall in the water. She tried to save him but she can't swim.

At 8 years old Janice and her father went to Yellowstone Park and were hiking together at an area far away from the beaten path. They stopped at a site overlooking the park. The edge had no guardrails and it was a sheer drop of 30 feet or more, Janice told her father to be careful and he told her, Oh' it'll be all right". Her father slipped and fell 30 feet, at the bottom he was on his back and couldn't move, he called out to Janice to go get help that he was hurt. Janice said she would and walked back out of sight of her father, set down and started eating their lunch. Meanwhile Robert was moaning and calling Janice name from time to time seeing if she had gone for help, Janice never said a word. After an hour or so a couple of hikers came by and Janice ran to them and told them that her father had a bad accident. Carla and Ken stop by the hospital where Robert was to see how he was doing. A broken left leg, broken nose and wrist and cracked ribs.

He said he'd live thanks to them, it

was a blessing that Janice found them when she

did. Yes, it was lucky wasn't it, Carla said.

After they left Ken said to Carla, you know if we hadnt been looking through our binoculars, we never would have seen that little girl sitting by herself underneath that tree eating and no one else around. And her father at the bottom of the cliff all the time, Carla said.

Why do you think she didnt go for help? Ken said. I don't know Carla said but I suspect that little girl has issues and she lies. Don't you think we should have told Mr Robert 'ken said? No! I don't. Carla said. We need to stay clear of him and that little girl, she's trouble and going to cause someone a lot of grief, and I believe he's in denial. We can do one thing for them, Carla said. What's that, Ken said? Pray for him and his wife.

At ten years old Janice had told her mother that she was having nightmares and whenever she do she wakes up wanting to hurt someone or something. Her mother told her everyone has nightmares and that she'll get over it in time. After telling her father, he felt the same. You'll get over it he said. At age eleven she went to visit her aunt Ronda in another state, a week after Janice was there the aunt tripped and fell down a flight of stairs and broke her neck, Janice cried for a solid week. At the funeral her mother just stared at her and would not speak to her.

One night Joyce told her husband what she suspected, and suggested they get her help. He got mad and told her he was ashamed of her for implying such a thing, and he didn't believe it. There was nothing wrong with their daughter and that would be the end of the conversation.

For two years after that they were family again but at her school in the gymnasium a teacher was found dead in the girl's bathroom. The police who investigated the incident said the teacher slipped and fell on a finger nail file and stabbed herself in the heart. An accident!

At the age of thirteen, girls club camp near ranch Memos, near the Deer Park area, she had her first lesbian relationship. A white girl of about 17 years and a counsellor, it wasn't the counsellors first affair. The affair lasted for the three weeks they were in camp, they never saw each other again after that. Another lesbian affair wooden take place for another ten years for Janice. But the nightmares were coming less and less.

In the school auditorium Officer Brad Miller a five year veteran of the Detroit Police Department was giving a lecture on police adequate to kids in the 7th and 8th grade, and how to better relate between police and the public.

 The police is your friend he went on to say, they want nothing better than to help you. After all, if a burglar breaks into your home who you gonna call? If you get carjacked, who you gonna call? If your bike gets stolen, who you gonna call? It's the police, and the police, and the police again. So you see we're not all bad, sure we have some rotten apples like all organizations do but we're not all bad. And we are trying to get these rotten apples out.

Lastly, when you see a police car driving by you might want to give them a wave to say hello and that you appreciate them.

Thank you, and I enjoyed talking to you. Go out and be good citizens!

After the session a few of the students went up to Officer Miller to ask him questions, Janice was one of those students. Suppose one wanted to join the police department, what classes would they have to take and are the department ready for women Officers? Miller went on to give her the spill he tells everyone and Janice knew right off it was a bunch of BS.

The only real reason she came up to him was that he was a nice looking man, a Hulk! For her age Janice was looking more like on 18-year-old, 5 foot 6, large long legs, large brown eyes, long nose, wide lips and milky white teeth. Almond colored skin and large breasts. Run track and played basketball, so Janice was in top shape looking like a supermodel but one with meat on her body. Ofc. Miller saw this right away.

And he was smitten by her. He knew that he couldn't say too much to her where they were so he gave her his card and suggested she call him if she wanted to know more about the program.

And it began!

Part 2

Meeting in the parks, her slipping out her bedroom window at night. Making love in the patrol car, more than once. Meeting at the beach and motel rooms.

And then the bad luck. Then her dad came down ill and he caught pneumonia and passed away. The next thing that happened was that she came up pregnant and told Brad, that's when she also told him that she was only 15 years old and he freaked out.

He took time off from his job to go hunting, so he said. Everyone knew that he had a cabin somewhere in the hills, no one had ever been there. A couple of days later he contacted Janice and asked her if she could get away and go with him. They had talked about doing this earlier and she said "sure, I can get away".

A few days after that Brad picked Janice up and they headed for the cabin. Once in the cabin he made a fire in the fireplace, cooked a nice dinner and they made love on the living room floor in front of the fireplace on the large pillow. Brad asked her if she would like a small drink and Janice said "sure, why not". Both were laying nude on the floor but when Brad tried to get up he couldn't move. What the hell, he said. Janice I can't move, that sex had to be something special this time but I really can't move.

I know she said, I thought the drug would have kicked in before now but better now than never. You see I spiked your drink when we were eating, I knew you would get to me soon after we ate and had sex, so you first.

But why Janice, why!

Let's not fool each other Brad, after I told you my age and that I was pregnant you started making plans for me then, that's when I knew you'd kill me because I was pregnant. You probably could have lived with my age but not my being 15 and pregnant. How long did it take you to figure out that I had to go? Not long I bet, it's only been less than two weeks since I told you.

What did you give me, Brad said?

Oh, just a little something I cooked up in the school lab, it works on the nervous system. You can move your eyes (even talk), everything except move your body. It will keep you that way for 5 hours or more, Time enough!

Then what Janice, then what? You gonna kill me. Once I get out of this situation just what do you think I'm going to do to you? Brad said.

Brad, what makes you think you'll ever get out of this situation?

What do you mean Janice?

What plans did you have in store for me Brad? That is other than killing me.

Killing you, where did you ever get that idea?

I did like you Brad, maybe even love you but I think you were right, it would have never worked. I'm going to miss you Brad, I will. I hope you're not attached to this cabin.

What do you mean Janice? Brad said. Because I plan to burn it down, with you in it. Janice was lying on her side looking at Brad and asked him if he really cared anything at all about her?

Well sure Janice, couldn't you tell.

Janice, don't do this. I'm due to get promoted soon, I'm gonna make Sgt.

Janice just stared at Brad and said, I gotta go!

Wait, Brad said. You not really gonna leave me like this? You not that cold!

Janice started getting dressed, put on her coat and walked over to where Brad had his wallet and took the cash out.

Janice, you joking right? Right!

Goodbye Brad, Janice said.

Janice looked back from the main road and saw the smoke. It was so dry that the cabin went up like the Forest in California. The location of the cabin meant that by the time anyone ever got to it, it would be too late. Brad started screaming for help once he was convinced she was really leaving and smelled the gas.

Well, so much for the myth of the bravery of the Detroit Police Department.

Next, the abortion!

A year later on her death bed Janice was standing over her mother and she asked her not to cry and to be strong. I've talk to your uncle and he's agreed to take you in, you shouldn't have to be with him long. You've had a good education and a good head on your shoulders, you should do well.

Mother, I'll be all right don't worry about me just get better.

Now Janice you know there's no chance of that, but I do want to ask you something and I hope, do to my situation you will tell me the truth. Will you tell me the truth Janice? What is it you won't to know mother, how can I put your mind at ease? Over the years her mother said. There's been many unexplained things that's been happening and you know what I speak of.
Whatever are you talking about mother, whatever you know in your heart to be true, trust your heart? But I'll tell you what you don't want to hear. I'm listening, Janise! Yes mother, I killed them, I kill them all. The kitten, the puppy, rabbit and

bird. My aunt, your sister. The policeman, my little schoolmate, gymnasium teacher and mother, I killed daddy.

But Janice could have saved her breath, her mother's eyes were wide open but she wasn't hearing a thing, she was dead!

But there was a horror on her face that she died with, the part she did hear put that look on her face. Janice was looking out the window with her back turned while telling her mother this and hadn't notice she had died.

I tried to tell you mother but you wouldn't listen, nobody listened!

After Janice's mother was buried and all the friends and relatives were gone Janice was left there in the house alone except for her uncle Bob. They were deciding where Janice was to live, the uncle said to Janice I'll be up front with you we've all heard the stories about you all your life and I for one believe them. I tried to get your mother and father to get you help but you know how that turned out. Your mother asked me to take you in after she's gone but in good Conscience I have to tell you, I can't do it. I have to think about my family. My wife and two daughters are still at home, we have a cat and a dog. I can't take the chance, I just can't take the chance.

I understand uncle Bob, Janice said. I really do.

Say, how about this.

Why can't I stay right here? I have the life insurance money that mother left me and the house is paid off. All I need is two years, and I'll be out of here and on my own. I'm on time to graduate so all I really need is for you to give your approval, or don't say nothing at all.

Now that may work Janice, uncle Bob said.

And it did, Janice stayed in her parent's three-bedroom home, she received a check every month From the Social Security Department until she turned 18. Enough to pay the utilities, buy food, clothes for school and all around upkeep for herself. She loved it.

Since that time with Brad she wasn't looking for anything like that for a while, the Brad incident turned out great. The only thing left of the cabin and Brad was bones.

The drugs were never thought of since his death was ruled an accident. They may have been seen a time or two but no one put it together. If they did, no one said.

She had no doubt that he intended on killing her, she just got to him first. I'll miss him she thought. She excelled at school she even came in number 1 and 2 in track and won a trophy.

Judo was one of her favourites and she did well there to. Her instructor thought she should try out for karate, that it would be a natural progression for her. But she decided to try out for kickboxing first.

Taking all these different classes would bring her home late some nights and since she still didn't own a car she would have to walk or take the bus. There was the long way and the short way which takes her through the park.

Sometimes she'd go through the park as she did this night. The park wasn't all that dark there were lights here and there just not enough. Since taking these classes one of her instructors had given her a gift of a Japanese throwing knife. He taught her how to use it and throw it, it was approximately 6 inches long, 3 inches for the handle and 3 inches for the blade. The blade was extremely sharp and had to be kept in a pouch which she wore in the middle of her back.

She love that knife and always practice in her backyard. This night she was in a hurry to get home, she had classes in both judo and kickboxing. She had to remember that was a little much, one behind the other like that.

Being November it got kind of dark early in Detroit and not many people were out. She once heard her aunt say "that was the best time to visit Detroit because that's when the rift wraps aren't out".

It wasn't so bad in the park this night she even saw a couple of kids roller-skating, but three quarters of the way into the park she thought she heard something in the brush.

She wasn't walking that fast but being on the safe side and hearing the noise again she picked up her pace. Her hands were in her Jacket pocket. Backpack was on her back and she tensed up just like she were about to enter a contest.

The 1st kid jumped in front of her and stood there, holding some kind of a club. He was a student just like her of about 17 years old, 5 foot 6 and 150 pounds, but not as tall as her. Janice stopped where she was and then she heard someone behind her and she turn her head in that direction. Another kid was there but this one a little larger. About 18 years old, 5 foot 10 and 175 pounds.

What do you want Janice asked, I don't have any money?

We don't want money but that may come later the big one said.

 Shit! The larger one said, you know what we want. They had picked one of the darkest areas of the park all you could see of them were there out lines and not a very good look at them at all.

I think you boys should go home and read a good book and forget about this Janice said.

 Boys! You'll find out who's the boy in about two minutes.

 Janice let her backpack slip off her shoulders to the ground and hooked her thumb in her back belt near the knife. The bigger of the two said, "Now Lawrence". Lawrence ran toward Janice and then the larger one ran toward her from the rear. Since the larger was the closest he got to Janice 1st. Janet had her knife out and when he came up on her she had turned around and was waiting for him. When he came up on her she swiped at his midsection with the blade and cut him wide open. He screamed, fail to the ground whimpering and holding his self. Janice turned toward the other who had seen his friend go down and he tried to stop but was too late. His momentum had run him into Janice and she swiped at his face. The blade caught him under his left eye and cut him down his cheek to his upper lip. The next cut was underneath his chin down his neck and into his chest. The little fella grab his face and screamed, turned around and ran, forgetting about his friend. The larger of the two was still lying on the ground holding his midsection and whimpering. Janice walked over to him put the blade to his left eye and moved it down the left side of his throat. He looked at Janice his eyes wide, Blood oozing out from between his fingers from holding his midsection and he urinated on himself. And said No! Please, No!

Janice cut him from the left side of his throat to the right, and she took her time. And she enjoyed it.

The next couple of days it was all over the school, a kid had been found murdered in the park. They found out he was from the school across town and couldn't figure out why he was in this neighbourhood Except to Rob someone. He was a top basketball player and due to graduate soon on a scholarship. They think a friend of his may have killed him, his name is Lawrence Johnson. They were as thick as thieves, where ever one went you'd see the other. As of now he is a person of interest they said.

Lawrence, what the hell happened to you, His brother Robert said?
I kinda got a little fucked up last night, me and Ron tried to take down this Bitch and ran into a bumblebee. She pulled a blade from somewhere and did this to me, I don't know what happened to Ron but I got out of there.
So, Robert said, you haven't heard the news?

Hey man, I've been ducking and hiding trying to fix my damn face. I think I'm gonna need some stitches, a lot of stitches.

You going to need more than that Lawrence, they found Ron this morning in the park with his throat cut.

Lawrence mouth dropped open and he looked at Robert in disbelief. No way, he said. I don't believe it! Well that ain't all Robert said, there looking for you for his murder.

What the fuck you talking about Robert, I didn't lay a glove on him and besides I was too busy running. Well all I know is that the cops are looking for your ass so you better think of something.

Got damn Robert, what can I do? The girl, it was the girl!

Let me ask you this Lawrence, what did you do to her to make her fuck you up like that? We done nothing Robert, honest!

Bullshit! Robert said. I didn't just get off the turnip truck, you two probably tried to molest and rob her and picked the wrong person.

No Robert, we tried but she was too fast for us, we never got the chance. We never touched her! Who in the hell's going to believe you, Robert said. Look in the mirror. If I was the cops I'd look at Ron "Dead" and I look at you, WA LA! I've got my killer.

No! No! I'm telling you that it was the girl that killed him. What should I do Robert? I'm fucked either way I go.

Chief Wilson called Detective Stevens to his office and asked him how he was coming along on the Park Murder Case, to which it was being known.

I can tell you what I know chief and that is the guy we found dead, Ron Harris. We thank was trying to rob someone in the park and it backfired on him.

He's been known for that before but he was never convicted. He always ran around with a kid name Lawrence but we haven't found him yet.

Do you know who they were trying to rob, the chief asked.

No, whoever it was didn't think it wise to stick around. We thank the person who had the knife knew their business because there's two sets of blood samples out there.

O/ positive and AB negative. There's one other thing, Ron was cut in the midsection 1st and then the person came over and cut his throat. The other guy that was with him we thank was Lawrence. On the other hand Lawrence and Ron could have gotten into a fight and Lawrence killed Ron. We won't really know until we pick up Lawrence. If they were trying to rob someone and they got the best of them, that's self-defence. But then there's Ron with his throat cut, which looks like murder to me.

Okay said the chief, keep me informed.

Two days later Lawrence turned his self in, he was interview charged with murder and released on bond.

Lawrence, his lawyer said to him. I'm not going to pull any punches with you, it don't look good. If that person that kill Ron don't come forward then you're it. But not to worry, I've got a man looking into what happened, if there was a girl he'll find her.

I hope so Lawrence said. I sure hate to go to jail for something I didn't do

Rob Morris, 35 years old, 5 foot 8, 210 pounds. X Air Force Sgt with a dishonourable discharge. Investigator for Roger McAllen law firm.

He had been working for Roger five years and they both have had a profitable relationship, even if they have gawk their clients a number of times.

Look Rob said. Why you taken this kids case, he don't have any money and he's probably guilty anyway.

That's true Rob but his parents has money, there sitting on a paid-up home and plus it makes me look good doing a pro bono every now and then. When you look into the case you don't have to put a lot of effort in it, just enough to show we're doing something. Even if he's telling the truth we know he's guilty of something so if he go down "oh well"

A week later Janice was in the kitchen warming her a can of chili when she heard a knock at the door, it was uncle Bob. Hi Uncle Bob how you doing, I was just about to have some chili, have some?

No thanks, I'm good Janice, I just stop by to see how you were doing.

I'm doing fine uncle, things couldn't be better.

Classes still on track for you to graduate? Uncle Bob said.

Sure is, I even have a scholarship in the making in track.

That's great Janice is that your plans, to go to college?

I'm not sure yet, college or the military.

I also see you are doing okay with your home utilities and things, I haven't gotten any feedback off your bills.

And you won't uncle, I'm on top of things.

I have a beer in the box if you want one.

Beer, how did you manage to get beer at your age?

Uncle, you know those old men that's always in front of the liquor store? Well I just give them a little change or buy them a bottle of wine and they purchase it for me. Would you like a bottle Janice asked again?

Well since you're asking"damn right." Janice and uncle set down at the kitchen table, she eating her chili and he drinking his beer.

It was small talk for a while, how the family was doing, missing her mother and father. The fun they use to have in the early years and so on.

Did you hear of that murder they had in the park a week ago uncle said?

Everyone heard about that uncle, I think they got the person that did it, didn't they?

Yeah, but they said in the paper he was let out on bond. I'll tell you Janice you have to watch yourself today, can't be too careful.

I try uncle, I try!

By the way, you been having any more of those bad dreams?

Not for a while, I think I've grown over them, dad said I would.

Part 3

Lawrence,

Was coming out of the doctor's office seeing about his stitches. The doctor informed him that if the blade would have been a half inch higher his eye would have been history. Be thankful that you only came out of it with less than 100 stitches, and yes you will have a scar. Come back in two weeks and we'll see how you're doing.

Damn Lawrence thought, my eye, that's all I need was to lose my eye. Fucking around with that Ron, I stay in the shit following him. Well, no more Ron he got dead. It's no doubt in my mind that the girl did it, thing about it I don't even know who she was. I wouldn't know her if she was standing right beside me. It was so dark out there I could hardly see Ron, but we had done the deeds so many times before and it worked, we just knew what to do. Once Ron said"now"I was to jump into action. Didn't work this time, this time we ran into a mother jumper. Ron's dead, I'm cut to hell and no one knows who the girl is. And to top it off I may go to jail for Ron's death. I'm in deep shit, if I manage to get out of this I'm changing my ways, I swear.

Rob went to the park where the assault happened to look around, there was quite a few people out but then it was the weekend. A few couples walking, people riding bikes young and old. Joggers and walkers, nice park really but he notice the lights and how they were spread. Too far apart he thought, at night that would be a problem for someone walking alone. He would have to come back at night and check it out. One other thing he asked himself, who would be walking through the park at seven or eight at night, so he decided to walk around to see what establishments were in the area. There were movies, barbershops, restaurants, pizza parlors, 7-Eleven stores and a high school. Any number of places the walkers may have been coming from. That had to be a hell of a young lady to take both of those young men down like she did. And to cut one of their throats," damn". She was one pissed off lady, if it's true.

Two weeks later in downtown Detroit at the Museum of art, schools from across the city was there visiting. Janice school was one of those. This was one of the last outings before graduation, Janice was taking notes and taking in whatever she could because of a test that was due the next day. Da Vinci, Rembrandt, Goya and Monet. They were all there and she really focused on a few and had hopes of a good paper. After being in the museum for 30 minutes or more on the 2nd floor she stopped in front of a Norman Rockwell portrait and begin taking notes. Beside her were other kids doing the same when she overheard, "hey Lawrence, what in the world happened to you?" You don't look so swell. I thought everyone heard about this Lawrence said. Ron and I were attacked in the park a couple of weeks ago, by some Looney Tunes. Ron was killed. Janice was listening to this and looked toward the kids. One had bandages down the left side of his face just underneath the left eye, on down his face into his chest area. Did they catch the ones that did this to you the one kid asked? No, not yet Lawrence said. But they're trying to lay it all on me.

 You and Ron were friends, wasn't you?

 Yeah, that's right, Lawrence said.

That's tough man, I hope things work out for you. Once the kids walked off Janice said to herself "so that's the other attacker". He would be a nice looking boy if he didn't have all those bandages on.

What did you find out Rob, Roger asked? The District attorney is about to indict Lawrence we need something to go with.

I walked the neighbourhood and talk to people, even walk through the park during the day and a weeknight. Now, I think Lawrence was telling the truth but we may have a time proven it. They have so many people using that park till you could take your pick who they confronted. There's moviegoers, schoolkids, judo classes and karate classes to name a few using that park. So to be honest with you Roger I just don't know. One thing for sure, Lawrence didn't cut his self.

If our person was a known offender it would be fairly easy but since Lawrence and Ron was the perpetrators the other person may never surface again.

So, let's go over it again, what do we have? Roger said.

Well, we think it's a female between the ages of 17 and 22, approximate height 5 foot 4 to 5 foot 8, 120 to 145 pounds, wearing pants and sweater with a backpack, what leaves me to believe she's a student. There's one school in that area that has over 3000 students, at least half of those being females. So your guess is as good as mine.

So what's next Roger said?

I'm going to make one more walk through the park at night just to put my mind at ease.

If we can't come up with anything Roger said. I'll just tell him the best thing to do is take a plea agreement and hope for the best. We losing too much money.

Janice had just finished taking her shower after training in her kickboxing class, the class held fifteen students all female. Five being Basic and Beginner up to black belt. This class is three nights a week and the top five have been together two or more years. The five also take judo or karate, run track. Two of the girls are Olympic bound. Janice and the other two are in it for the Adrenaline. After their shower Janice and two of the girls stopped at the ice cream parlor before they went home. Janice and one of the other girls (Scarlet) live close to each other and they decided to walk through the park after. You know Scarlet said, we may get molested walking this way.

 They wouldn't dare mess with us Janice said. With what we know!

Both girls were wearing pants, pull over sweater and sneakers, both had backpacks. Halfway through the park a male approached them and ask them if he could speak to them a moment.

 I don't know Janice said, what do you won't? And who are you?

I'm Rob Morris an investigator for the law firm of Roger Mc Allen. I'm investigating the murder that happen in this area the other week.

So what do you want to know, Janice asked?

 I wanted to ask you do you take this route home every night and did you walk home the night of the murder. Basically, did you see anything?

Look Janice said. We told everything we had to say to the cops that came around so maybe you should ask them.

Scarlet said, for all we know you may be the assailant.

I assure you I'm not and I do have identification Rob said.

We come this way most every night Scarlet said, sometimes alone and other times in groups. We never saw anything and the only thing we heard is what everyone else heard. That two guys tried to molest a girl and she beat there asses. Isn't that right Janice?

That's what I heard Janice said, and if so sounds like poetic justice to me.

So how many girls walk this path at night like you two Rob asked?

A lot Scarlet said.Comming behind us you'll see maybe twenty more, alone and in groups. The last class ends about 9 PM.

Okay girls, well thanks, if you think of anything, and he handed them his card, please call me. After the girls left Rob thought"damn those are some fine young things "wonder what they're feeding them these days. They sure didn't look like that when I was going to school. If Ron and Lawrence saw something like that no wonder they tried to make a hit on them. Shit, I'm getting horny now myself.

A week later Janice woke up at about 12:30 in the morning, her head was throbbing and her eyes felt like they were rolling out of their socket. Fingernails seem like they were growing longer, skin growing taunt and mouth and teeth growing longer and out of their sockets. Her body was shaking out of control and she felt she had to hurt somebody, anybody. She got out of bed, put on her jumpsuit with her sneakers, a dark blue jacket and her Japanese throwing knifc and walked out the house.

The next day at school Scarlet approached her and asked her about the killing last night in the park? Had she heard? Janice said she hadn't and Scarlet went on to tell her what she heard.

A male student was walking through the park when a person attacked him and killed him for no reason they said. They didn't take his money or anything like that but get this, they cut his throat, just like that Ron boy. Look like we got ourselves a serial killer, wouldn't you say Janice?

Sounds like it Janice said. I guess we won't be walking through the park anytime soon.

Does this mean the person they have is off the hook Scarlet said.

I don't know about that Janice said. Who's to say he didn't do that kill to?

Yeah, you may be right scarlet said. He may be in deeper DO DO.

Rob, have you heard? They had another killing in the park last night.

Do that let our boy off the hook?

That depends Roger said, if he has on alibi or not, we better get him in here.

I'll call him and see if I can reach him Rob said. If not I'll go to his house. I'll also go to the park and see what I can pick up over there.

At that moment Detective Stevens of the Detroit Police Department called and asked Roger did he know where Lawrence was?

Roger said he didn't, he's also looking for him.

Detective Stevens said they went to his house but he wasn't there. His mother had stated he left the house after he received a phone call and she hadn't seen him since and that was earlier this morning.

It don't look good for him, Stevens said.

Well he hadn't contacted me Roger said.

If he do I'll let you know.

He needs to come in Detective Stevens said, we need to talk to him.

That was Detective Stevens, Rogers said to Rob. They tried to pick up Lawrence but he had flown the coop.

What can we do now Rob said?

We can't do a damn thing until he contact us, I'll call his mother and tell her that if she hears from him that's what he should do. I have a feeling this is not going to end well.

After getting the word that another body was found in the park Lawrence felt he should hit the road, there was no way the authorities would believe he had nothing to do with it, especially with no alibi.

He had a few hundred dollars stashed under his floorboard in his bedroom so he collected that and headed for the bridge crossing over to Canada. Once there he would head for Alaska. Since he had no transportation he had to get there the best way he could, so his first stop was the bus station. There he had enough money to get to Fairbanks, and there he could hitchhike up the Alaskan highway to Anchorage.

Just like hitchhiking anywhere you would get rides off and on, he spent many nights on the side of the road, good thing he had purchased supplies such as a sleeping bag canned goods, cold weather gear etc.

Or he wouldn't be able to make it. Good thing he was from a cold climate his self. What he really wanted was a pistol but wasn't able to acquire one. Oh well, what the hell, I got my freedom.

300 miles up the highway Lawrence accepted a ride from two men driving a 7 year old, long bed pickup truck, with a toolbox on the back.

Both men wear Parker's and the typical Alaskan hats. One was tall and blonde the other short and stocky, beards that cover most of their face except their eyes.

Lawrence was kinda reluctant to get in the vehicle but had no choice who he rode with, there was not a lot of traffic headed in his direction. Besides it was getting near dark and Anchorage was still over 500 miles away.

We're only going about 50 miles down the road to a cabin we have but tomorrow we're going on into Anchorage, you're welcome to ride along one said. Well I got nothing better to do and no other prospects Lawrence said. Sure I'll ride along, thanks!

The cabin was two miles off the main road, a shed out back. No bedrooms, just one big open space. Fireplace and sink, two windows and two bunk beds with a dirt floor. Sorry kid but you gonna have to sleep on the floor, the Tall one said.

No problem, Lawrence said; I've been sleeping on the ground for the past two weeks now anyway.

Slim (let's call him that) started a fire and shorty started putting out the bacon, beans and coffee for dinner. After eating shorty brought out a bottle of Moon Shine, Slim retrieved 3 cups and fill each one to the brim.

I have to tell you Lawrence said, I'm not much of a drinker.

Well, maybe not kid but you have to have one drink with us, that's the code of the Yukon.

Now, the first one will be straight down the hatch, Shorty said. The second one half that, and then the third, well, the third you can do what you want with it.You won't be feeling a thing after that anyway.

Okay, Shorty said. Down the hatch! After the first cup Lawrence was out cold.

Okay Shorty said; who goes first? You want to flip a coin for him or pull straws?

Part 4

Rob was obsessed with finding the killer because he just didn't believe Lawrence kill them. He had made a large turnaround, from when they had first started, now he thought just the opposite.

Running didn't help his case any and he's been gone now about 3 weeks and no one's seen hide nor hair of him.

The cops are still looking for him, Roger and his family are also looking for him, no Lawrence. Right now he's their main suspect.

Rob has been going to the park off and on for 3 weeks now at all times of night till 3 in the morning but no luck.

A couple of nights he's ran into other cops with the same idea. This night, a Thursday at one in the morning he thought he'd try his luck. He had been at the club drinking and was on his way home more than a little tipsy, when he had a hunch. Thirty minutes after getting there and walking around he heard it, a tussle in the brushes between someone near the main path. When he came upon two people, one was on top of the other stabbing them a number of times when he called out"hey"and ran up behind the perpetrator and kicked them off the victim. The perpetrator rolled off the victim and came up on their feet like a train Acrobat, turned around and faced Rob with the knife in their hand and started toward him. Rob was thinking, maybe he shouldn't have stopped off at that club. He put up his hands in a defensive stance but he knew in his condition he had no chance against the person he faced. Plus he had left his weapon in the car.

The perpetrator swung at him with the knife and cut his outstretched hand and Rob started bleeding. Another swipe and the other hand was cut. Rob felt he wasn't getting anywhere doing what he was doing so he decided to attack the person as if he was back on the football field. He was surprise how easy it was to take them down; Rob landed on top and tried to grab the knife hand and for a minute he had it, with his hand being wet with blood a couple of things happen at once. His hand slipped off the knife hand, they knee him in the groin and turn him over on his back in one fluid motion, landing the person on top of him. If he didn't know any better he'd swear it felt like a female on top of him. The wrist, the way he took her down, how agile they were. If it wasn't for the circumstances he just about got an erection. And then he hesitated, for just a second. The knife reached his throat and swiped, the blood sprayed out like it was a water fountain. The blade entered the neck again and while there it was turned counter clockwise. Rob had a brief glimpse of the person that was over him and he thought for one split sec. "I know this person"

He shivered, arched his back, closed his eyes and died.

The next day;

Mr. Mc Allen, this is Detective Stevens, I'm afraid I have some bad news for you? Your investigator Rob Morris was found dead this morning in the park, we thank it was the same person that kill the others.

I can't believe that Detective, I just saw him yesterday. He said he'd be going to the club last night but lately he's been obsessed with the park killings and been patrolling their a few nights a week seeing if he could get lucky.

Well, he could have been right, be size him being killed there was also a woman that was killed. What we surmised is that he walked up on the killing and tried to help and got dead for his effort.

You know Detective, Rob wasn't no slouch in the combat department but if he just left the club that could have made the difference. Are we going to call this a serial murder now? Roger said.

I think so Mr. Mc Allen but that isn't my call.

Where is Rob now, Roger asked.

He's at the morgue, he'll have to go through an autopsy, and I'll let you know.

How in the hell could they get the upper hand on both, Roger asked? And you still don't know if it's a man or a woman do you?

No we don't, but I'll tell you one thing, there someone to deal with if you ever run into them, Steven said.

Any info on Lawrence yet, Roger said? He should be off the hook now, wouldn't you say detective? I would think so unless he came back to kill the last two. If he don't come back or call in we'll never know. And again Mr. McAllen, I'm sorry for your loss.

Breaking news:

Again a body was found in the Central Park area, this time two bodies were found. One male and one female, both were killed by knife. The female was stabbed all over her body and the male was stabbed in his throat. The male was the investigator for the lawyer who was accused of killing Ron Harris, the first person killed in the park. We have had four murders so far, there is a serial killer lose in the city of Detroit.

Where is Lawrence Johnson? The authorities are still looking for him. Maybe he has 3 more kills to his credit.

Janice are you excited about our graduation coming Scarlet said. And what about the class going to Florida for our break.

Oh, I love it Janice said. It'll give us a chance to get out the city. Plus I've never been to Florida and a week there, I can handle that. I'm so tired of hearing about all these murders I think all of us could use a change.

Are you going to keep up your kick boxing after graduation Scarlet asked?

I don't know Janice said. I haven't decided what I want to do. One thing for sure is to get the hell out of Detroit.

Janice, look there!
Coming out of the principal's office was Detective Stevens and one other. I wonder what's that all about, Scarlet said.
You can just about guess, Janice said. The murderers! They'll probably be all over the place now, I heard they were over at the Karate

Academy the other day. Look like they're pulling out all the stops, Janice said.

I don't know why there questioning the students, we wouldn't have anything to do with any murders, Scarlet said. Remember that investigator they found dead, I think he was the one that approached us. I wonder if the police would want to know that.

If they asked us then we'll tell them, Janice said. Once they think we know something they'll never leave us alone, may even keep us from making our trip to Florida.

Detective Stevens? This is Capt. Ramose of the Alaskan state police. You have a warrant out for a man named Lawrence Johnson? Well he's in our jail or hospital you might say, you got a minute?

Sure do Capt., how long have you had Lawrence and what happen to him?

We've had him about three days now, actually we picked him up by chance, we were going after two other men that we had warrants for and there was Lawrence.

Was he staying with the men or what, and how in the hell did he get all the way to Alaska. Stevens said. Well it's like this detective when we broke in on our two and started searching the place there was this shed out back.

When we opened it up there was Lawrence naked as a jay bird and tied to a makeshift something, out of the dark ages. He was laying over this thing with his ass pointing toward the moon and behind him was one of the men, with two cans of Vaseline beside them.

The reason they never heard us come up was that Lawrence was screaming his head off. His body had Cigarette burns, and belt marks all over him.

He was a mess, eyes swollen, nose broke and lips split. We had to call on ambulance for him. As far as how he got up this way, I have no idea. But I'll tell you this, he sure ran into two bad dudes. We been searching for these guys for a couple of years now, your boy is not the first.

Damn Capt. that don't sound too good for Lawrence, if we want to come get him when will he be in any shape to travel? Steven said.

I'm no doctor detective but I'm thinking somewhere around thirty days or more, and there is one other thing. After you get him I don't think he'll ever be right again, in the head I'm talking about. He's really fucked up.

Look Capt. about how long would you say they held him?

Two weeks or more I'd say. We'll find out for sure later on. You could say on the other hand he was quite lucky.

How so Capt?

They've killed all the others they held hostage. Let me know what you want to do, whenever you want him he'll be here.

That was some bad luck for Lawrence but it proves he didn't have anything to do with our last two victims. He should have stuck around and fought the system.

Hey, what are you doing on this part of the beach and this time of night, I thought I had this spot all to myself.
You see what thanking will get you Janice said.
What are you doing this far up the beach?
Oh I come up here to relax and get my thoughts together, many people are not aware of this area and they don't like to walk this far. What's a girl like you doing this far aren't you afraid? It's awful dark out here.

No, I'm not afraid Janice said. There is a full moon out and you know what they say about fear.

Say, I've got some wine over here why not sit and have a cup. By the way, my name is Phil.

I think I would love some wine Phil, thank you, Janice said.

Scarlet came into Janice room and asked her if she was packed yet? Janice said she was and they went down the motel stairs to the waiting cab.

That was some kind of a vacation wasn't it Janice? I think most of it was a blur for me. Drinking, dancing and screwing. Damn, I couldn't do this every day Scarlet said.

What happened to you Janice? We didn't see you much at all.

You know me Scarlet, I found me someone and we laid up all week. I could have stayed another week, she said.

A week later after returning from Florida and graduation Janice was walking through the mall, she passed a military recruiting office and stopped. She looked at the posters for the Army, Navy, Air Force and Marines. While there a representative of the Army and one for the Air Force came out and spoke to her trying to convince her to join their branch. She had told both that her mind wasn't made up yet and she'd be back.

At the footlocker Janice ran into Scarlet and among other things she told her about a killing on the beach in Florida the night before they left. Janice asked her how she be knowing all this stuff.

I listen to the world news every night, you can ask me anything and I'll probably know it, that is if it's happened within the last week or two. You want to get something to eat?

Two weeks later Detective Stevens received a call from Capt. Ramose.

I just wanted to inform you that there's no need to pick up Lawrence anymore you can take him off your wanted list.

Why Is That Capt?

At 3 AM this morning Lawrence Johnson jumped out of the 7th floor hospital window, and Committed suicide.

He did leave a suicide note for his mother, you want to hear it?

Why not, Steven said.

"Dear mom, you were right all along. The things I did to others come back to bite me. Everything you warned me against came true, I should have listened. One thing I want you to know is that I didn't kill Ron, he was my friend.

I love you mom and I'm sorry."

Your son, Lawrence

At that moment Janice was being inducted into the United States Air force.

I, Janice B. Willow, Do solemnly swear...

www.ingramcontent.com/pod-product-compliance
Lightning Source LLC
Chambersburg PA
CBHW061454170626
46811CB00004B/1506

* 9 7 8 0 9 9 0 5 4 4 0 9 8 *